BASED ON THE NOVEL BY P. L. TRAVERS

MARY POPPINS

Houghton Mifflin Harcourt
Boston New York

Adapted by
Amy Novesky

Illustrated by
Genevieve Godbout

hmhco.com

The illustrations were created with soft pastel and colored pencil.
The text type was set in Fairfield.
The display type was set in Kiddie Cocktails.

ISBN 978-1-328-91677-8
Special Sales ISBN 978-1-328-63400-9

Library of Congress Cataloging-in-Publication Data is on file.

Manufactured in China
SCP 10 9 8 7 6 5 4 3 2 1
4500718146

If you are looking for Number Seventeen Cherry Tree Lane—
and it is likely that you are, for this book is all about this
particular house—you'll find it.

Four children live here.
Jane, the oldest,
Michael, her brother, and the twins.
The family's nanny had left unexpectedly,
and it was bedtime.

Outside, the East Wind blew, howling through
the cherry trees that lined the street.
The wind madly spun Admiral Boom's weathervane.

Michael joined his sister, Jane, at the window. The twins were howling as loud as the wind. And that's when they saw a strange shape flying toward them.

It was a woman, carrying an umbrella in one hand and a bag in the other.

The wind seemed to fling her at the house, where she landed heavily against the front door, quieting even the twins.

"I've never seen that before," said Michael.

Neither had their parents, for they promptly opened the door.

At the top of the landing, the children watched as this curious visitor flew up the banister. Jane and Michael slid down the banister all the time—much to their parents' dismay—but never up!

Despite the wind, she was as neat as a pin.

There was something exciting about her.

"I am Mary Poppins."
"How did you find us?" asked Jane.
"The wind blew me here," she said.
And then Mary Poppins wasted no time
getting settled.

She removed her hat, set down her umbrella, and from her strange bag she pulled out . . .

a starched apron, which she tied around her waist

a bottle of scent

a box of lozenges

a set of dominoes

two bathing caps

seven flannel nightgowns

four cotton ones

a large bar of soap

a pair of boots

a toothbrush

a pack of hairpins

a postcard album

"Now spit-spot to bed!" she said.

And before they knew it, Jane and Michael, and even the twins, were put in their pyjamas, bathed and brushed and read to, much to their parents'—and their—delight.

"Mary Poppins, you'll never leave us, will you?" asked Michael.

"I'll stay till the wind changes," she said.

From that night on, Mary took charge, and the children followed.
    And every day with Mary was an adventure.

    They always waved to Miss Lark, their next-door neighbour,
on their way out.
    "Good morning! And how are we today?" she said.
    Jane and Michael never knew if she was asking how *they* were,
or how she and her spoiled, fluffy, little dog were.

They always stopped to admire the Match-Man's work. On sunny days, the Match-Man made chalk drawings on the sidewalk instead of selling matches.

"Strike me pink!" Mary always said when she was pleased.

On this particular day, Mary Poppins, Jane, and Michael were taking the bus to pay a visit to Mary's uncle, Mr. Wigg.

"Why is your uncle called Mr. Wigg?" asked Michael. "Does he wear one?"

"He is called Mr. Wigg because Mr. Wigg is his name," said Mary. "And he doesn't wear one. He is bald."

Inside Number Three Robertson Road,
an enormous table was laid for tea. But where
was Mr. Wigg? Jane and Michael heard a giggle
and looked up.

"Oh, Uncle Albert—not *again!* It's not your birthday, is it?"
Mary Poppins asked.

"I'm afraid it is my birthday," he said. "And whenever
my birthday falls on a Friday, well, it's all up with me.
Absolutely U.P."

"Why?" asked Jane.
"How?" asked Michael.
"Well, you see, the first funny thought and I'm up like a balloon. And until I think of something serious I can't get down."

The children laughed, and the more they laughed, a curious thing happened. Jane felt herself growing lighter and lighter. It was a delicious feeling, which made her laugh more. Then Michael started laughing too.

But Mary Poppins liked to be proper. "Really!" she said. "Really, *such* behaviour!"

"Come up, Mary Poppins!" cried the children. "Think of something funny!"

But Mary didn't need to. She could fly even without laughing. She brought the table with her.

"Time for tea!" announced Mr. Wigg.

And the children laughed some more.

"It's time to go," said Mary after a while, and—no need to think about serious things, like school or growing up— they all came down with a thump. Just in time to catch the bus home.

When the days started growing shorter, Mary Poppins brought
Jane and Michael to the most curious shop they had ever seen.
  "Fannie! Annie!" Mary called out in the empty shop.
  "Annie! Fannie!" Her echo called back.

Miss Fannie and Miss Annie appeared with their mother, Mrs. Corry. "How de do?" she said with a dreamy smile.
   She offered Jane and Michael a baker's dozen of gingerbread, each adorned with a gilt paper star.

Arms piled up with the delicious dark cakes,
Mary and Jane and Michael headed home.

Later that night, after the gingerbread was gone and they had hidden their gold stars away in the nursery, Jane and Michael awoke to voices outside the window.

Fannie and Annie each held a ladder, and set them up with one end on the earth, the other in the sky. Mrs. Corry painted the sky with glue. And Mary Poppins stuck gilt stars that began to twinkle furiously.

Their stars!

"Are the stars gold paper or is the gold paper stars?" Jane wondered.

But she knew that only someone very much wiser than Michael could give her an answer.

Another bedtime, on a cold winter night,
Michael was thinking about elephants.
    "I wonder what happens in the Zoo at night."
    "Spit-spot to bed you go!" said Mary Poppins.
    "She knows everything, but she never tells,"
Jane whispered.

Just as they were about to drop off into sleep, they heard a voice say, "Hurry!"

Jane and Michael followed the voice out of bed and down the Lane, across the park, until they came to the Zoo.

In the light of the full moon, Jane and Michael saw the most amazing thing: The animals were free! In the center of it all was Mary Poppins.

The voice belonged to a bear wearing a coat with brass buttons. He handed them each a ticket and told them:

"We are all made of the same stuff. Bird and beast, star and stone—we are all one."

Winter turned to Spring, as it does, and the bare cherry trees on Cherry Tree Lane blossomed and rained pink petals once again.

Mary Poppins was especially quiet as she tidied up after supper. For a moment, she put one hand lightly on Michael's head and the other on Jane's shoulder. There was something different in the air.

Admiral Boom's weathervane
confirmed: the wind had
changed.

Jane and Michael heard
the front door slam.
They rushed to their
bedroom window.

Jane and Michael opened the window.
"Mary Poppins!" they shouted.
    The wind blew her over the rooftops,
and away from Cherry Tree Lane.
    Would they ever see her again?
    "Au revoir!" she called.
    Which means, Dear Reader,
"to meet again."